Martin Waddell

Napper Strikes Again

Illustrated by Barrie Mitchell

Puffin Books

A book for anyone who remembers
HOLMAC F.C.
Where are they now?

Puffin Books, Penguin Books Ltd, Harmondsworth, Middlesex, England
Penguin Books, 625 Madison Avenue, New York, New York 10022, U.S.A.
Penguin Books Australia Ltd, Ringwood, Victoria, Australia
Penguin Books Canada Ltd, 2801 John Street, Markham, Ontario, Canada L3R 1B4
Penguin Books (N.Z.) Ltd, 182–190 Wairau Road, Auckland 10, New Zealand

First published 1981
Reprinted 1983

Made and printed in Great Britain by
Richard Clay (The Chaucer Press) Ltd, Bungay, Suffolk
Set in Linotype Baskerville

Contents

1   Up for the Cup   7

2   Red Row Stars v. Morth Heath Youth   12

3   Raven Boys Club v. Red Row Stars   33

4   Training   48

5   Red Row Stars v. Abbey Villa   55

6   Red Row Stars v. Morth Park   71

7   Tactics   81

8   Skye Blues v. Red Row Stars   87

9   A New Challenge   107

Red Row Stars F.C.: Summary of   108
Appearances and Goalscorers

Football Notes   110

This is the Red Row Stars First Team Squad:

Top row (L. to R.): C. Small   Avril McCann   D. Forbes
M. Bellow   S. Watts   T. Prince   J. Ramsey
S. Rodgers   P. Scott   D. Wilson
Bottom row: H. Haxwell   J. Small   J. Deacon
N. McCann (Capt.)   D. Rooney   H. Brown

1. Up for the Cup

My name is Napper McCann. I am the Captain and leading goalscorer and so I am holding the ball. The one who is holding the bucket and looking sick is Cyril Small. He has a broken leg. You can tell that he has a broken leg because it is in plaster. His plaster leg has all our names written on it and some jokes like 'HELP, I AM A PRISONER IN THIS PLASTER'. Our schemer, Harpur Brown, is the one with the black eye and the hair. The tough-looking one is Harry Haxwell, the one with the bandy legs is Dribbler Wilson and the goalie is our Player-Manager, Terence Prince. The one who looks like Dracula is my horrible sister Avril McCann, who shouldn't be in the picture because she doesn't play football.

The day after term started, John Deacon came into the P6 and P7 room and said, 'The Baboon has called a special football meeting in the hall after school. All footballers to attend I.Y.D.W.A.C.B.'

'What does I.Y.D.W.A.C.B. mean?' asked

Marky Bellow, who isn't very bright although he is in P7. I am in P6. I'll be in P7 next year.

'IF-YOU-DON'T-WANT-A-CROSS-BABOON!' shouted everybody else.

The Baboon is Miss Fellows, who helps us to run our football team. She isn't like a baboon but her hair is.

'Yah! She's going to stop football and go shopping on Saturdays instead!' said Ugly Irma Bankworth.

'Go hide your head in a bucket, Irma,' said Cyril.

'Best place for it,' said Harry Haxwell.

'You won't be laughing when she says no more football,' said Ugly Irma.

The trouble was, we thought she might be right. There had been no football team at Red Row School until I thought of having one. I told Terence and Harpur Brown and Cyril Small, and we asked Mr Hope, our Headmaster, if we could start one. He said we could if the Baboon would help us, and she said she didn't mind giving up her Saturday mornings to supervise if we took it seriously and didn't fool about.

That was last term. Now the new term had started and we were going to have an emergency meeting where Miss Fellows would tell us she couldn't go on with the football. That's what we thought, but when we got down to the hall Miss Fellows said, 'I've entered your team in the

Barnleck and District Spring Cup. First match Saturday on the rec.'

Everybody started cheering and dancing about except Harpur Brown who said, '*What* Cup, Miss?'

'Barnleck and District Spring Cup,' said Miss Fellows. 'You're playing Morth Heath Youth on the rec. on Saturday. Group B.'

'We're going to win the Cup! We're going to win the Cup!' Cyril started chanting.

'We thought we'd be in the Primary Schools, Miss,' Terence said.

'We're too late for the Primary Schools this term,' Miss Fellows said. 'I was sure you'd want some proper competition instead of friendlies, so I got in touch with the Barnleck League Secretary, and you're in the Spring Cup!'

'We are the Champions! We are the Champions!' Cyril and Dribbler Wilson and John Deacon and the others were jumping about and shouting. I felt like jumping about and shouting myself because it meant that I might be playing in a Cup Final almost at once, and getting a Cup Winner's Medal.

'Are there medals, Miss?'

'Plaques, I think,' she said.

'We're on our way to Wembley!' Cyril shouted. He was waving his arms around, showing off the Cup we hadn't won yet, when he accidentally punched Scuddy Rodgers in the mouth.

9

'Cyril!' said Miss Fellows. Then she shut everybody up and explained to us how the competition worked.

There were twelve teams entered in the Spring Cup, and they had been divided into two Groups of six teams each. Each team played the other teams in its Group once, and at the end the two teams with most points in each Group went into the semi-finals. The winners of Group A had to play the runners-up in Group B and the runners-up in Group A played the winners of Group B.

'We're in Group B, so that's us!' said Cyril. 'We're on our way to Wembley! We are the Champions! We are the Champions!'

'Cyril, ENOUGH!' said Miss Fellows, looking at him fiercely over the top of her big blue glasses. Sometimes she *does* look like a baboon.

'We're going to win the Cup, Miss,' said Cyril.

'Who else have we got to play, Miss?' asked Terence.

Miss Fellows read out her list:

BARNLECK AND DISTRICT YOUTH LEAGUE
SPRING CUP: GROUP B

Red Row Stars	Morth Heath Youth
Skye Blues	Morth Park
Raven Boys Club	Abbey Villa

'We'll beat that lot easy,' said Cyril.

'I bet you get stuffed,' said my sister Avril when she heard about it.

'Don't say "stuffed", Avril,' said Mum. 'It's rude.'

'Pulverized, then,' said Avril.

I didn't say a thing. She would smile on the other side of her spotty face when I came home with my Winner's Plaque!

BARNLECK AND DISTRICT
YOUTH LEAGUE
SPRING CUP: GROUP B

FIXTURES

Red Row Stars v. Morth Heath Youth
Skye Blues v. Abbey Villa
Raven Boys Club v. Morth Park
All results to be communicated to the Match Secretary, 231 East Drive, Morth Park Estate by 8 p.m., Saturday.

---

2. Red Row Stars v. Morth Heath Youth

BARNLECK AND DISTRICT YOUTH LEAGUE
SPRING CUP: GROUP B
Red Row Stars v. Morth Heath Youth
Referee: K. J. Stallard
Venue: Rec. field, Barnleck

Morth Heath Youth were all about six foot tall and super-fit-looking and they had four footballs and a trainer in a track suit. They came from the estate in a minibus with MORTH HEATH YOUTH CLUB in big letters on the side.

They had white shirts, white shorts and black socks. They were jumping about and doing ball exercises and saying our pitch on the rec. wasn't up to much.

'They're big,' said Terence.

'The bigger they are, the bigger they splash!' I said, because I'm the Captain and I'm supposed to cheer everybody up. I didn't feel very cheerful. I had colly-wobbles because it was our first-ever match in a real competition. I should have known they would be big, because Morth Heath is one of the largest estates in Myreton and they have the whole place to pick from.

'It's a good thing we've got Harry back in the team,' said Cyril, who had been boasting about winning the Cup all week, but wasn't looking so confident now.

This was the team for our first-ever proper competitive match in the Barnleck and District Youth League Spring Cup against Morth Heath Youth:

T. Prince

P. Scott   C. Small   H. Haxwell   J. Deacon

S. Watts   H. Brown

S. Rodgers   N. McCann (Capt.)   J. Small   D. Wilson

Substitute D. Forbes

Travelling Official Miss E. Fellows

The only change in the team was Harry Haxwell coming back. Miss Fellows had suspended him from our last match for bad behaviour, but she said he could play again in the Cup, so that was all right. Harry is one of our strongest players. It meant that Duncan Forbes was out of the team, so he became substitute instead of Mark Bellow, who came along to hold the bucket.

Although we had only one different player from our last big match against St Gabriel's School, we had switched people around. With Harry playing at the back, we were able to bring Harpur into the midfield where he could link up with me. Then we decided to switch

Scottie Watts and John Deacon, because we wanted to stiffen up the left-hand side of the defence. John isn't big, but he is quicker than Scottie, and the idea was that Cyril and Harry in the middle would cope with the high balls and John would dash about tackling and wouldn't be caught easily on the turn like Scottie.

Terence told us all what our jobs were. He told me to look out for one-twos off Joe Small and Harpur, if Harpur could get far enough upfield to make that work.

'Our best team,' said Terence, when he stuck it up on the board.

'Puddins!' said Ugly Irma, which is just like Ugly Irma. She should have been forming a Supporters' Club or something, but she wasn't. She just went around calling us names. All the girls did, except Helena Bellow who wanted to play. We thought she might be a better player than her big brother Marky, but that wasn't saying much.

The referee blew his whistle and I went up to toss. He was a proper ref with a badge and black shirt and shorts and a whistle. Marky Bellow was our linesman and Morth Heath's trainer was the other linesman. Miss Fellows looked after Morth Heath's four footballs because their trainer was afraid that their supporters would kick the balls into the ditch at the end of the rec. field.

Their Captain was about twice as big as me.

'Haven't you kids got proper jerseys?' was the

first thing he said to me. 'You lot don't half look crummy!'

Our world-famous Red Row Stars grey jerseys were old school shirts with red numbers sewed on. It was Terence's idea when we hadn't got jerseys for our team.

'All the teams in this league have proper jerseys,' their Captain said. 'Silly-looking, not having jerseys!'

'It's the way we play that counts,' I muttered.

He called, because it was our home game, but I won the toss and decided to kick into the High Road end, which meant that they had kick-off.

They kicked off and I ran forward and tackled their inside man. The next minute I got a terrific dig in the ribs from his elbow as he crashed past me. He played the ball out to the left-winger who was another six-footer, almost. The inside man came walking back and as he passed me he said, 'Watch it, Titchy Boots, or somebody is going to get hurt!' Then he kicked me on the ankle.

'Hey!' I shouted, but he had sprinted off, grinning all over his freckled face. The ref didn't see it, so I was left with a sore ankle.

Morth Heath had gone straight down to our end and they started firing in shots at Terence. First he caught one at the bottom of the right post, and then he had to tip one over for a corner. When the corner came over, a big red-headed boy called Derek ran straight at Terence and collided with him as Terence went up for the ball.

Terence ended up holding his stomach and lying on the ground, and the ball was nestling in the back of our net!

'Great goal, Derek!' they all shouted. They started jumping up and down and mobbing the redhead, but the ref said it wasn't a goal and he gave us a free kick.

Harpur took the free kick and he played it across field to Dribbler who had moved back.

Dribbler took the ball and turned neatly inside his man who had come charging up to challenge him.

BANG!

Dribbler was down, holding his leg, and the back had booted the ball towards our goal and was charging after it like Avril when she sees our Dad with sweets.

The whistle went.

Another free kick to us.

'Powder puffs, you lot,' grumbled their centre-half, and he spat on his hands.

He was big, much bigger than me, with a mop of fair hair and a broken nose. He was chewing gum, and he looked as if he ate P6s for breakfast.

The ball came over. I got up over him despite the tug he gave my shirt, but it took me off balance enough to spoil my header, which their goalie caught easily. I ran in and stood on his right side, blocking his clearance.

'I'll smash your face!' he said, and he banged into me. The ref's whistle went.

I thought I had got a penalty or an indirect free kick, but instead the ref came running up and said, 'Get back, you. No interfering with the keeper or you're off! Just watch it, son!'

I went back down the pitch red in the face. I hadn't been interfering with their keeper at all. We were getting kicked all over the place, but I was the one threatened with being sent off!

Harry Haxwell showed them they weren't the only ones when he took the ball off Freckles with a magnificent slide tackle and then bundled the one they called Bonkers into touch down by the corner flag.

For a moment I thought that there was going to be trouble, because their trainer ran on to the pitch and started waving his flag and shouting. In the end, the ref gave a free kick against Harry.

We moved back for the free and Bonkers started backing into Harry. I think Harry would have done something then, but Cyril shouted, 'Watch it, Harry! He's playing for a penalty.'

Harry gave a nod and moved back with Bonkers treading backwards after him. They looked like a pair of Siamese twins, joined together. Harry looked as if he wanted to thump someone, preferably Bonkers. Harry had come on to the field wanting to prove to everyone that he was our best defender because he was still mad at having been kept out of the St Gabriel's game. Now Bonkers was stepping backwards on to his toes, just waiting to fall over in the penalty area and yell, 'Foul, ref!' We were all waiting for Harry to lose his temper.

'Okay, Harry,' Cyril said, coming over to him. 'You take Freckles. I'll do this one.'

'I'm stayin' where I am,' Harry said, and he wouldn't budge.

I saw Derek giving the thumbs-up sign to Bonkers. They were pleased because they'd got one of our defenders mad. They were hoping that Harry would upset the rest of the defence.

The ball came over high and Harpur, Terence and Derek went for it together; but this time Harpur kept Derek from laying Terence out. This picture shows him doing it:

It was all right, but the trouble is that you can give away a free kick for obstruction that way if you are not careful. Morth Heath were very keen on playing for free kicks! When Terence got the ball, big Derek said something to Harpur and I thought that the ref would pull him up, but he didn't.

Terence threw the ball to Scottie Watts who booted it upfield. Little Joe Small got the ball and was smacked flat on to his face by Chewing Gum, who came in from behind. The ref didn't blow. The ball went down the field and their inside-left, who was their smallest player, waltzed round Cyril and fired in a fierce shot that Terence palmed up in the air but couldn't hold. Harry Haxwell got back just in time to turn the ball away for a corner before Derek thumped into his back. Harry turned and looked at him hard. Big Derek walked away. He started clapping his hands and shouting, but I didn't think he would go near Harry again.

The corner came over and Derek came storming in. Harpur and Terence were watching him as the ball drifted high over the goal, waiting for him to thump into them. They were so busy watching Derek that they didn't notice Freckles who cut in front of everyone, rose like a bird and headed the ball down into the bottom corner of the net past Peter Scott who was supposed to be covering the post.

Harpur and Terence stood glaring at each

other. They had both been so busy looking out for Derek that they had missed Freckles altogether, which was just what Morth Heath wanted them to do. Playing kick-the-keeper seemed to be paying off!

1–0 to Morth Heath.

'They're playing rough to try and knock us off our game,' I said to Harpur.

'Trouble is, their plan's working,' Harpur said.

Then we went on to the attack.

Almost at once we got a free kick on the edge of their area when Dribbler was kicked by the back again. He was a long time getting up off the ground, and when he did he was limping.

Harpur came up to take the free kick and gave me Secret Sign Number 7.

Our Secret Signs stand for tactical plans for dead-ball situations. Harpur and Terence worked them out and we've spent a lot of time in the playground practising them.

Morth Heath lined up to block the shot, looking huge in their white shirts. They left Chewing Gum lying just to the goalside of the wall and behind it, to pick up anyone coming through.

Harry moved up behind Harpur when he saw Harpur rubbing his left leg, which is Secret Sign Number 7.

The whistle blew.

I ran at the ball and jumped over it. Then I went left, past the end of the wall, running straight at Chewing Gum and the goal. The man at the end of the wall moved to go with me, bringing the man next to him with him.

Harpur ran up, touched the ball sideways, and ran at the wall, veering to the right. Some of the Morth Heath players started forward, some of them wanted to follow Harpur, and the gap we wanted appeared.

Harry hit the ball like a rocket but he missed the gap.

The ball smacked against Bonkers and spun up in the air over the wall. I saw it had beaten the wall and I went after it. Chewing Gum had lost me altogether. The ball was dropping between me and their keeper. He came crunching out and lunged at me, feet first. I got my head to the ball and it crashed into the net just before his boot sank into my side.

GOAL!

A great goal! Our first ever in the Barnleck and District Youth League Spring Cup! Here I am scoring it:

1–1!

'Little twerp!' said Chewing Gum.

'Twerp yourself,' I said, rubbing my side where the goalie's wild boot had gone in. I started to limp back towards the centre, with half our team trying to jump on my back to show what a super goalscorer I was. It didn't help the pain! But I didn't mind – I'd scored a goal. Or I thought I had! The ref was waving at me and blowing his whistle as if he was a one-man band.

I went over to him.

'I've already warned you once, son,' he said. 'Lay off the keeper!'

Chewing Gum was placing the ball in their goal area. The ref had given a free kick against me for going in on the keeper.

'Ah, ref!' I protested.

He blew a long blast on his whistle and started wagging his arms like a windmill. Then he pulled out a pencil and pad from his pocket.

I was booked!

'I'm the ref in this game, son. Just you remember it, or you'll get an early bath!' (Actually, there weren't any baths in the changing-rooms, but I knew what he meant all right.)

It was a fifty-fifty ball and the goalie had tried to scythe my legs off short at the kneecaps by coming in feet first where the ball wasn't . . . and they got a free kick because I was supposed to be playing dangerously! What made it worse was the way Derek was pummelling Terence every time Morth Heath got into our penalty area.

It was 1–0 to Morth Heath, not 1–1. We had been robbed by the ref!

'Don't risk it again, Titchy Boots,' Chewing Gum said as their goalie went to take the free kick. I moved back to cover against a break, and as I did so Freckles trotted past and gave me another swift tap on the ankle.

'Ouch!'

I went blazing after him, fists up!

'Ref! Ref!' Their linesman was dancing on the field, shouting and pointing his flag at me.

Somebody grabbed me round the middle and forced my arms down. It was Harpur.

'Okay,' I said. 'But they're bashing me every time I turn round.'

'I'll swap bruises with you,' said Cyril, who had come over to stop me punching Freckles and getting sent off.

Morth Heath got another goal before half-time when Bonkers trod all over Peter Scott and got in a shot that squeezed by at Terence's near post. It was a good shot, but we should have had a foul.

Here is the goal:

2–0 to Morth Heath.

'You want to watch it, son, throwing your weight about,' their trainer said to me as we were coming off the field at half-time.

The Baboon came up, looking furious.

'Napper! Harry! What do you think you're doing out there?' she snapped. And the next moment she was telling *us* off for kicking *them*.

'We're getting kicked all over the place, Miss,' Cyril said. 'Morth Heath are going for Napper and Harry because they're the two players with the bad tempers!'

'Who do you think you're calling bad-tempered!' I said, turning on him, absolutely blazing with anger.

'Napper!' Terence grabbed me.

'Look, Miss,' Harpur said, and he rolled down his socks. There was a great big bruise on his right leg, and a dribble of blood. Then Terence showed her the marks on his stomach and ribs where big Derek had got him, and Dribbler showed his bruises and Scottie tried to show his, but he had kept so well out of trouble that he hadn't got any.

'I've a good mind to stop the game and call you all off!' she said, when we had convinced her that we were the ones who were being kicked.

'No, Miss,' we all said.

'I'm going to give that referee a piece of my mind!' The Baboon is good when she goes all mad but we persuaded her not to. It wasn't the ref's fault that they were a dirty team, though he was a bad ref. If he had been a good one, he would have spotted what Morth Heath were up to.

'2–0 down,' said Cyril. 'We're not going to win the Cup this way, are we?'

'Yes, we are,' said Terence. He was still annoyed about the two goals, and all the crosses he had been missing. The first goal was his fault, and the second was a near-post goal which always annoys good goalies. He was annoyed, but he hadn't wasted his time trying to punch people. He had thought up another of his emergency plans.

When we lined up for the second half, 2–0 down to Morth Heath Youth, we had a new centre-forward.

Harry Haxwell!

The idea was this. We were 2–0 down, so we had to attack. If we didn't score at least two goals, we would lose anyway. So Terence moved Scottie Watts back into Harry's place and left the defence for Cyril to organize. I moved back into midfield with Harpur, but the idea was that I would poach behind our forwards and Harry would run around up front and take the thumping I had been collecting, hoping to lay the ball off where I could nip on to it and get one back.

'We've got to keep you away from the keeper, Napper,' Terence said. 'If the ref sees you anywhere near him, you'll be off. This way, there's no risk of Harry giving away a penalty at the other end either.'

Trouble was, it left us with a weak defence because keep-out-of-trouble Scottie Watts was no substitute for Harry.

We didn't worry about that. Straight from the kick-off Harry started laying into Chewing Gum, who wasn't pleased to be up against somebody his own size. Harry gave as good as he got. It wasn't pretty, but it wasn't dirty – not on Harry's side anyway. We had all warned him about the danger of being sent off. The first time Chewing Gum chopped him, Harry just walked away; and the next time Chewing Gum lunged in, Harry switched feet as if he was Dribbler Wilson, and then pulled the ball across to Super Shot Napper McCann who was sprinting up on a late run from the back. The Morth Heath team hadn't worked out who was marking who after our reshuffle, and so I was in the clear when I reached the ball.

WHAM!

I hit one of my Super Great Smacking Swervers and the goalie just watched it crashing into the net behind him.

You can see from the diagram what a neat pass Harry gave me, and how their defenders were caught out by my late run:

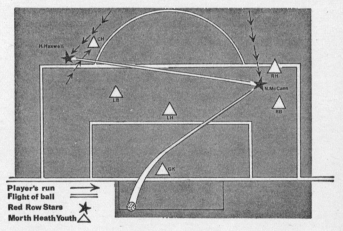

Player's run
Flight of ball
Red Row Stars
Morth Heath Youth

2–1 to Morth Heath Youth.

Chewing Gum didn't like it.

The next time the ball was played down to them he smacked into Harry's back – hard!

The whistle went.

Penalty!

I'm Captain and leading goalscorer, and

normally I take all the penalties myself because I'm our Super Shot. But I didn't want to take this one.

I gave the ball to Harry.

'Huh?' he said, gaping at me.

I don't get on much with Harry. He didn't fancy me for Captain because I was in P6, and he said I was only Captain because I was Terence's friend and not because I had thought of having the team, which is the real reason. He thought we were always ganging up against him and I wanted to show him that we weren't. He'd given me my goal and I reckoned he deserved one himself.

It was a good idea. There was nothing fancy about Harry's penalty. He hit the ball like a rocket and almost broke the net!

2–2!

'Not so smart now, are you?' I said to Chewing Gum. They had spent the first half trying to annoy Harry so he would give away a penalty, and instead Harry had moved up front and annoyed them into giving him one.

As the game went on, Morth Heath started to give away a lot of free kicks. Either the ref had got wise to them or they were getting wilder after seeing a 2–0 lead change to 2–2.

There were about five minutes to go when we got our break!

They were up around our goal and Peter Scott managed a long toe-punted clearance which bounced in front of Joe Small. Joe did the only thing he's good at, which was to play a quick first-time ball back towards Harpur. Harpur played a deadly accurate ball downfield to Harry, who was racing in on the edge of the Morth Heath penalty area. Chewing Gum came puffing in like a stone-crusher and the pair of them went down in a pile of arms and legs. The ball broke free in front of me.

Three strides and I had it. Everybody was shouting for a penalty and half their team had stopped, but I kept on going and cut into the area. Their goalie came out feet first again, not minding whether he got me or the ball. I showed it to him, shoved it past him, hopped over his arms as he tried to bring me down, and tapped the ball into the net!

3–2 to Red Row Stars!

'We are the Champions!' Cyril shouted.

Morth Heath went on the attack in the last few minutes, but we seemed to have everything tied up. We all came back and defended and there was no danger until suddenly Bonkers came bursting through on his own and Terence had to rush out to head him off. Somehow Harpur cut in between them and tipped the ball off Bonkers' foot. He chased it across our goal and saw big

Derek closing in on him, so he thought he would make Derek look silly by back-heeling the ball to Terence.

Harpur back-heeled the ball in front of our goal and it rolled slowly into the net.

3–3.

'Oh, great goal!' said Terence in disgust. He had rushed out to dive at Bonkers' feet, and ended up in a tangle on the ground when Harpur beat them both to the ball. 'First you take it off me when I had it covered, then you back-heel it home!'

'You wouldn't have got to the ball before Bonkers,' Harpur said.

'I would.'

'You didn't call,' said Harpur.

'And you didn't look to see if there was anyone in goal before you back-heeled, did you? What a rotten place to back-heel anyway, in front of your own goal!'

They were still grumbling at each other when the final whistle went.

Red Row Stars 3, Morth Heath Youth 3.

'Wembley here we come!' shouted Cyril. We were all pleased at getting a draw when we had been 2–0 down, even if we should have won. 3–3 seemed a good result against a team of players who were much bigger than we were. All the teams couldn't be like that.

'If you ever come down our place, we'll kick

your kneecaps off!' Chewing Gum grunted to me as we walked off the pitch.

I don't know how it happened, but somebody kicked one of Morth Heath's four footballs into the ditch.

'Who did that?' said Miss Fellows.

'Wasn't me, Miss,' said Harry Haxwell, looking happy.

BARNLECK AND DISTRICT
YOUTH LEAGUE
SPRING CUP: GROUP B

FIRST SERIES RESULTS
Red Row Stars 3   Morth Heath Youth 3
Skye Blues 6   Abbey Villa 2
Raven Boys Club 3   Morth Park 2

GROUP TABLE

Team	P	W	D	L	F	A	Pts
Skye Blues	1	1	0	0	6	2	2
Raven Boys Club	1	1	0	0	3	2	2
Red Row Stars	1	0	1	0	3	3	1
Morth Heath Youth	1	0	1	0	3	3	1
Morth Park	1	0	0	1	2	3	0
Abbey Villa	1	0	0	1	2	6	0

FIXTURES
Morth Park v. Abbey Villa
Morth Heath Youth v. Skye Blues
Raven Boys Club v. Red Row Stars

Home Team Secretaries are reminded that it is the HOME TEAM'S RESPONSIBILITY to communicate match results to the Match Secretary, 231 East Drive, Morth Park Estate by 8 p.m. Saturday.

3. Raven Boys Club v. Red Row Stars

BARNLECK AND DISTRICT
YOUTH LEAGUE
SPRING CUP: GROUP B
Raven Boys Club v. Red Row Stars
Referee: A. Smith
Venue: Starrett Common Sports Ground

Our second Group B match was against Raven Boys Club at Starrett Common.
Our team was:

T. Prince

P. Scott   C. Small   J. Deacon   M. Bellow

N. McCann (Capt.)   H. Brown

S. Rodgers   H. Haxwell   J. Small   D. Forbes

Substitute D. Rooney

Travelling Official Miss E. Fellows

The biggest change was Mark Bellow in the back four, and nobody was happy about that, not even Marky. He was in the team because of what happened at school on Monday after our game against Morth Heath Youth.

We were in the P6 and P7 room when the

Baboon came in looking grim and said that Mr Hope wanted to see Terence and Harpur and me. We went with her to Mr Hope's office.

Mr Hope inspected my sore leg and Terence's ribs where Derek had banged into him, and Harpur's leg.

He shook his head and looked angry. 'Well, Enid?' he said.

We didn't know the Baboon's name was Enid, but it was.

'I wanted them to have something to play for,' she said. 'I suppose it may have been a mistake. Of course, we shouldn't put too much emphasis on this one game.'

Mr Hope raised his eyebrows and then said that we boys could go.

That afternoon Miss Fellows talked to the Selection Committee – Terence and Cyril and Harpur and me – and said that we would have to have Mark Bellow in the team on Saturday; we couldn't have Dribbler Wilson because he had hurt his leg.

'What about Daniel Rooney, Miss?' I said. Daniel had just come back to school after having measles.

'We'll think about Daniel next week, when he's had time to settle in again,' Miss Fellows said.

So we had to play a really important match without Dribbler, which didn't please anybody. Then Scottie Watts rode his bike into the canal and he couldn't play either. Our sub, Duncan Forbes, took Scottie's place, and Miss Fellows said we could have Daniel Rooney as our new sub because there wasn't anybody else. That was all right since it meant that we could bring Daniel on, and Miss Fellows couldn't say anything because she had said he could be sub, and you can't have a sub who isn't allowed to play, can you? Really it was a good thing because Daniel is a much better player than Scottie Watts any day, but it didn't make up for having to play Marky.

Ugly Irma told us she had seen Mark's dad at the rec. on Saturday, and we reckoned he had complained to Mr Hope about Mark not being in the team when people smaller than him were in it. We weren't pleased.

We went down to Starrett Common with Mr Hope driving the minibus we had borrowed from St Gabriel's, because we aren't a big enough school to have a minibus of our own. Mr Hope said he wanted to see us win this time, and we hoped we would. We were third equal in the League, and if we won we would go top.

'We must be good if we're equal third,' said Cyril.

'Third equal out of six,' said Peter Scott.

'If we win we have three points, and if Skye Blues lose we'll be top equal!' Cyril boasted.

'Let's win this one first, shall we?' said Mr Hope.

Raven Boys were already out on the pitch when we got there. They had red shirts like Manchester United and they were bigger than us, but not as big as Morth Heath Youth. Their star player was called North, and we knew about him because Joe Fish of St Gabriel's had told us to watch out for him. North was their striker.

They kicked off.

Straight away they attacked us down Peter Scott's side of the field. They had a winger they called Squirt, and every time he got the ball he kept showing it to Peter and then turning him inside out. I had to drop back to help him.

I didn't do much good.

'Leave him, Pete,' I said. I went in hard with one of my Napper McCann Super Crunchers and he flicked the ball over my foot and got clean away. Pete came across late. The little winger beat him easily and drifted the ball inside to North, who got up above Cyril and headed a perfect goal into the top corner of the net.

Terence hadn't a hope of reaching it. He didn't look cheerful when he picked the ball out of the net.

1–0 to Raven Boys.

Five minutes later they got their second. One of our attacks broke down and their goalie cleared the ball downfield to where I should have been if

I hadn't been running forward trying to score goals. Squirt took the ball forward and then played a long high ball into the middle. It was a great ball because it was flighted well over Cyril's head, and North ran on to it like a steam train and hit it a terrific smack into our net.

2–0 to Raven Boys.

'Huh!' said Harry. 'I'm dropping back. This is hopeless. They can't stop anything back there.'

So he went back, and I moved John Deacon into Marky's place and Harry into the middle beside Cyril. I went into the front line, and Marky went to play alongside Harpur. I thought it was a good idea because Harry was too slow to make any impression on their defence, and I reckoned that I could nip in and score some goals from my best position, centre-forward.

They got a corner, and North went up and forced Terence to make a great save down by the foot of the post. Here is Terence making it:

It was a great save, but I was worried because I thought Terence should have come out for the corner in the first place.

The next time, Terence obviously made up his mind that he couldn't risk another rocket header, so he came dashing out for Squirt's corner and Harpur came rushing in and *bang*! They crashed into each other. North got in his header, but the ball hit Marky Bellow who was standing on the line. Old Marky woke up in time to swing his boot at it and hit it straight back the way it had come, right into Terence's hands. I don't know who was more suprised, Terence or Marky. I *do* know that Terence was mad at Harpur for crashing into him. He hadn't forgiven him yet for giving away that stupid goal in the last game.

North had another header, and Terence palmed it against the crossbar and it came down. Squirt made a dive and connected with his head, and Terence somehow got up for it with one hand and pushed the ball in the air. It dropped behind him right in front of their left-winger who looked at it as if it was a pudding, swung his leg and missed completely. He was standing beside old Marky and Marky was so surprised that he missed it too. The ball was rolling in at the post when Terence made his third wonder save in a row and put the ball away for a corner.

'Fantastic, Terence!' everybody said.

'Great save, keeper!' said North.

Terence has to play in goal because he has asthma and can't run far. His asthma doesn't stop him being a super goalie.

Squirt took the corner. The ball came over and Terence came rushing out, misjudged it and punched it into his own net.

'Might as well not have bothered, your keeper!' North said with a grin as he trotted past me on his way back to the centre.

3–0 to Raven, and that is how we stood at half-time.

'What about getting me on?' Daniel Rooney said, bouncing up to me as we came off the pitch. 'I was supposed to be substituted the first time anyone got kicked.'

I'd forgotten about Daniel. Nobody had been kicked, so there had been nothing to remind me, and I was too excited to think about substituting people when the game was on. I felt silly because Daniel might have made a difference.

'Okay,' I said, and I went up to Marky Bellow and told him I was putting Daniel on.

Mr Hope came up and I told him what we were doing. He said I would have to pull one of the small ones off. 'We need big players at the back,' he said.

'Marky's no use, Sir,' I said.

'Seems to me Marky didn't do so badly,' said Mr Hope. 'He saved a certain goal.'

I didn't say anything. We had to have Marky in the team because Mr Bellow had complained. Marky didn't really save us a goal. The ball just hit him when he happened to be standing on our goal-line getting in Terence's way.

It had to be Scuddy Rodgers, Duncan Forbes or Joe Small to come off. Duncan had been trying hard and Joe Small is a good passer and most of the time Scuddy had been standing around waiting for someone to pass to him, so I took Scuddy off. He went very pale, but he gave his jersey to Daniel. It didn't fit Daniel, but that made Daniel look bigger.

We were three goals down, so we had to attack. I put Daniel into the forward line in a straight swap for Scuddy. Daniel can run very fast and it meant I had somebody else to pass to.

'Bringing on your secret weapon?' North said when he saw we had made a change.

'We're not beaten yet,' I said. 'Wait and see what happens.'

We went straight into the attack. Harpur moved upfield, and in the first ten minutes we got into the game more than we had right through the match. I think that Raven thought they had the match won and they could afford to ease up a bit. We set out to show them that they couldn't.

First Harpur put Daniel away down the wing. Daniel beat their full-back to the ball and I went dashing into the penalty area, but Daniel shot into the side netting. Then Harpur got clear on the left and centred to me and I got a header in. Their beanpole goalie made a good save but he couldn't hold the ball, and little Duncan Forbes rushed in and got his foot to the ball, trying to force it over the line. The ball hit the inside of the post and ran across the goal-line and their full-back just beat Daniel to it.

The ball went down the field and their winger booted it on, but old Marky for once wasn't picking daisies. He got the ball and passed it forward to Joe Small. Joe pushed it inside and Cyril beat North to it and slipped it back to Joe. This time Joe was in the clear. He kept on running and actually beat one of their men. The Beanpole came rushing out of goal and smothered the ball but it broke free and Daniel dashed in and had a shot which almost hit the corner flag.

'Pass, Daniel. Napper was free!' Harpur shouted.

'Okay, okay!' Daniel said.

Cyril beat North to the goal kick clearance and this time he passed to me. I hit a spot-on ball behind the back. Daniel got inside and tried a shot when he shouldn't have, but the ball struck the centre-half and went for a corner.

Secret Sign Number 11!

All our big players went up for the corner. Harry and Cyril went into the area and Harpur

41

moved towards the far post. Their defenders didn't know who to mark.

I stayed on the edge of the area, at the side the corner was being taken from, which is where I was supposed to be for Secret Plan Number 11.

Harry and Cyril kept edging about the box, and there was a lot of jostling going on as the defenders followed them. Even big North went back, but that only made things worse.

Daniel took the corner. He shaped to take an in-swinger, but instead he hit the ball hard in my direction.

Too hard.

Instead of being able to pick my spot, I had to volley it and hope.

The defenders were caught out because they had been jostling and banging on the line, expecting the in-swinger.

I hit the ball on the volley, but I didn't get over it and I skied the ball. The ball went across the goal, beat everybody and slammed against the top corner of the woodwork. Then it spun up in the air and Harpur and the Beanpole both went for it and the Beanpole punched it out. It ran to the edge of the area where big Mark Bellow was standing. Marky saw it coming for once. He swung his leg and hit a massive toe-punter towards the goal.

It was a wild shot, but it went like a rocket right into the top corner of the net!

GOAL!

Marky Bellow had scored a Super Goal!

We all dashed over and lifted him off the ground, and he put both hands above his head and everybody thumped him on the back.

We were back in the game at 3–1, with a real chance of winning.

Here is a picture of how we got our goal, showing how the Raven players didn't mark me properly because they were so busy watching Harpur and Harry and expecting an in-swinger:

3–1, and we were back in the game.

Everybody got excited because we began to pile attack on attack, and it looked as if we must score again. The trouble was that their goalie was having a great game.

'How long, ref?' I asked.

'Ten,' he said.

I got the ball on the halfway line and squared it to Harpur and he played it back in front of me. I beat the full-back and saw Harry Haxwell moving up to the far post. I lofted it over to him and Harry came in like a jet plane and headed it into the net.

'GOAL!' we all shouted.

3–2.

But it wasn't!

The ref said that Harry had punched the ball instead of heading it, and gave a free kick for hand-ball.

'Did you head it?' I asked.

'Naw,' said Harry. 'It was going over my head.'

So he'd mucked up a great chance!

It was still 3–1 and we were running out of time.

'You can't all go upfield you know,' Cyril said a minute later, after he had managed to head off a long run by North. 'I want somebody back to help.'

Nobody would go back except John Deacon. Even Mark Bellow kept turning up in their half, hoping for another chance to toe-punt.

We got a corner and Daniel went across to take it. This time it really was an in-swinger, but their goalie called to his defence to leave it and he neatly took the ball off my head. I ended up in the back of the net with the ball drifting down towards Cyril from the keeper's clearance.

I don't know what happened to Cyril. Perhaps he didn't keep his eye on the ball, or perhaps it hit something. Anyway, instead of clearing the ball, he let it bang against his knee and break away from him to Squirt. Squirt booted it on and he and John Deacon started a desperate race for our goal.

Our goalie, Terence Prince, is no dozer! He saw what had happened and he started out like a flash.

CRUNCH!

Terence got to the ball first, but John Deacon came crashing into him, head down, feet flying. His boot caught Terence above the ear and Terence went down. The ball bobbed out of his hands, Squirt got a foot to it and the ball was in our net!

4–1 to Raven Boys!

'Terence should have called,' Daniel said to me. 'It was his ball.'

Terence was lying on the ground, holding his head. Mr Hope and Miss Fellows came running on, and the next we knew Terence was going off.

'There goes the match!' said Harpur, and he was right.

Harry put on Terence's green jersey and only let one more goal in, which wasn't his fault.

North got away from Cyril and whammed the ball in while we were still pushing players forward to try to get goals.

5–1 to Raven Boys.

That was how it finished. We had been badly beaten when we might at least have made a draw of it.

'Brilliant goal, Marky,' I said, as we came off.

'Reckoned I could lob him,' Marky said, and he trudged on, looking very pleased with himself.

'It might easily have hit the corner flag,' Cyril said, watching him go.

'Daddy's boy,' said Harry.

BARNLECK AND DISTRICT YOUTH LEAGUE

SPRING CUP: GROUP B

SECOND SERIES RESULTS

Morth Park 2   Abbey Villa 4
Morth Heath Youth 2   Skye Blues 6
Raven Boys Club 5   Red Row Stars 1

GROUP TABLE

Team	P	W	D	L	F	A	Pts
Skye Blues	2	2	0	0	12	4	4
Raven Boys Club	2	2	0	0	8	3	4
Abbey Villa	2	1	0	1	6	8	2
Red Row Stars	2	0	1	1	4	8	1
Morth Heath Youth	2	0	1	1	5	9	1
Morth Park	2	0	0	2	4	7	0

FIXTURES

Red Row Stars v. Abbey Villa
Skye Blues v. Morth Park
Raven Boys Club v. Morth Heath Youth

Will Home Team Secretaries PLEASE endeavour to communicate match results to the Match Secretary, 231 East Drive, Morth Park Estate by 8 p.m. Saturday. Failure to comply is IMPOLITE and causes delay in communication of results to the Press.

4. Training

Mr Hope came into our class on Monday and said he wanted all the footballers for training!

'Sir, Sir, please Sir, who's going to train us?' Cyril said.

'I am,' said Mr Hope. 'You can't go on losing matches 5–1, can you? If we're going to have a team in this school, it's got to be a good one!'

Everybody started cheering.

'Sir, Sir, will we have tactical talks?' asked Harpur, when everybody had stopped.

'Yes,' said Mr Hope.

'Ball training?' said Cyril, bouncing up and down as if he was a ball himself.

'Basic skills to begin with. *Like keeping your eye on the ball, Cyril,*' said Mr Hope.

'Heading?'

'Dribbling?'

'Basics,' said Mr Hope. 'Basics, basics, basics! Stick to basics!' And off he went.

'I didn't know that Mr Hope knew anything about football, Miss,' said Terence to Miss Fellows.

'He couldn't know less than me, could he?' said the Baboon.

Mr Hope had told us our first training would be on Wednesday, after school. On Wednesday everybody was there except Scuddy Rodgers, who said he didn't want to play any more.

'That means we'll have Dribbler in the team for Saturday,' said Terence when he saw Dribbler practising with Harry and Mr Hope. Mr Hope had a blue tracksuit on like a real trainer, and he was showing Dribbler how to shield the ball and showing Harry how *not* to tackle from behind.

'Maybe we won't give away so many free kicks now,' Cyril muttered.

We all stood round and watched.

This picture shows Harry tackling Dribbler from behind in his usual way, which would have been a foul if it happened in a match:

'Wrong!' said Mr Hope. Then he tackled Dribbler himself. You can see that, although he came from behind Dribbler and played the ball from the side, he was playing the ball and not the back of Dribbler's legs.

'If you go on doing it your way, Haxwell, you'll break somebody's leg,' said Mr Hope.

Then he showed Dribbler how to shield the ball with his body so that Harry couldn't tackle him without giving away a foul after all. Here is Dribbler doing it:

'Now then, attend! Two things can happen. If the defender lunges in at you, you get a foul; or

you time your own move so that he commits himself to come on, and you slip the ball away as he
lunges. What should Haxwell do as defender?'

'Lay off him, Sir,' said Cyril.

'Lay off him and . . .?'

'Tackle as he turns, Sir!'

'Right! Good boy! And what should the
attacking team do if the defender lays off?'

'Run into space so that Dribbler can pass, Sir,'
I said.

'How? Wilson has his back to the opposing
goal. He'll have to turn to make the pass, and
when he does the tackle comes in.'

'Sir, Sir, behind him, Sir,' said Terence.

'That's right. Basics! Wilson has to pass the
ball the way he is facing. He taps it back; one
of you has moved into the space behind him. He
turns.

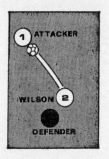

'If the defender goes with him, the player with the ball has a clear run.'

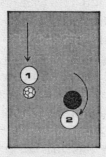

'If the defender follows the ball, the player receiving the ball from Wilson plays it forward again, past the advancing defender, and Wilson is in the clear.'

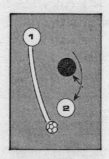

'Another great goal for me!' said Dribbler.

'But what should the defender do, Sir?' asked Harry.

'Try not to kick either of them, Haxwell, that's the first thing!' said Mr Hope with a grin. 'It depends whether he has cover or not. But don't dash in. That is just what the attacking side wants you to do. You can't go far wrong if you stay between the man you are supposed to be marking and the goal, and force the attackers to run across you. If they run at you, you must tackle eventually, but by then your cover should have arrived. Never commit yourself to following the ball away from goal unless you feel sure you are going to get it. The ball must go past you if the other team is going to score, remember that. Unless, of course, all this is happening within close range of goal. Then you will have to tackle to prevent a shot.'

Then he put five defenders against five attackers, and he put Harpur and Daniel Rooney out on the wings and asked them to swing the ball into the goalmouth.

'Drop some short, but hit some high ones as well. Vary it! This is an exercise for the defenders. Particularly you, Prince. You have been giving away goals by not calling properly when you're coming for the ball. You are the boss in the goal area. Make a lot of noise. Tell the others when you're coming out.'

So he had Terence shouting and rushing off his line to cut out crosses and through balls, with me trying to get to them first and Harry and Cyril breathing down my neck. I got three goals but Terence got most of the balls.

'Good,' said Mr Hope. 'I want you to go on practising that.'

He did tackling and covering back with Joe and the little ones, and more tackling with

Marky Bellow and Scottie Watts and Peter Scott, who don't usually do much of it in a game!

'Put your body in the tackle,' he said. 'The player who puts in half his weight is the one who gets hurt.' Scottie looked a bit doubtful about that and wanted to stop because he said his back was sore. He had hurt his back falling off his bicycle into the canal. Mr Hope said he should try to keep going if he wanted to be in the team on Saturday. Five minutes later Scottie almost broke my leg, so I don't think his back was too bad.

We all thought our training was great and we thought we would probably win our next match, which was against Abbey Villa, because we would have our full team out, including Daniel and Dribbler Wilson and Scottie. Abbey Villa were one point in front of us, and if we could beat them we would be third in the table with three points. If we then beat Morth Park and Skye Blues, we could finish second in the Group and we would be in the semi-finals against the winners of Group A.

'I bet your soppy football team won't win a single game,' my sister Avril said when I told Dad about it at tea.

'Wait till Saturday,' Mum said.

'You get a hat-trick, son, that'll show her!' said Dad.

'Oh sure,' I said. 'Dead easy, that is!'

5. Red Row Stars v. Abbey Villa

BARNLECK AND DISTRICT
YOUTH LEAGUE
SPRING CUP: GROUP B
Red Row Stars v. Abbey Villa
Referee: S. Ormskirk
Venue: Rec. Field, Barnleck

This was our line-up for the home game against Abbey Villa, who were one point ahead of us in Group B:

T. Prince

J. Deacon   C. Small   H. Haxwell   S. Watts

M. Bellow   H. Brown

D. Rooney   N. McCann (Capt.)   J. Small   P. Scott

Substitute D. Forbes

Trainer Mr Hope

Travelling Official Miss E. Fellows

No Dribbler Wilson!

'Dribbler should be in the team,' everybody said, but Mr Hope said we had to have Marky Bellow instead.

'He's a goalscorer, after all!' Mr Hope said.

Then Terence said we would pick Marky for the team if Mr Hope said we had to because he was big, but couldn't we have Dribbler as well, and drop Peter Scott who is not much use, or Joe Small who isn't much bigger than Dribbler?

'Joe's all right,' Cyril said, because he didn't want us dropping his brother.

'He's small, though, isn't he?' Terence argued. 'We have to play the big players. So that means we have to have Peter Scott and Marky and Scottie Watts. But we could drop little Joe and make him sub, and Dribbler could play in the team.'

Mr Hope wouldn't let us.

He said Joe Small was a good passer of the ball, which he is, and he said it would be better if Dribbler wasn't even sub.

'It isn't our rotten fault, Dribbler,' said Terence when he put the team up. 'We all think you should be in the team, but Marky's rotten dad complained about small ones and Mr Hope must think you're the smallest so you're out.'

'We told him you were good,' said Harpur.

'It's our team,' grumbled Harry. 'I don't see why we have to have Mark in it. He knows he's no good.'

'He's been practising,' I pointed out. 'He's been out in the yard every day this week.'

'His rotten dad should have kept his nose out of it.'

56

'It wasn't his dad,' said Dribbler.

'What?'

'It wasn't his dad who complained. It was *my* dad.'

'Why was your dad complaining about Marky not being in the team?' Harry asked suspiciously.

'He wasn't,' said Dribbler, going red. 'He only said Mr Hope should make sure we had big players in the team, not . . . not ones like me. He saw my leg after I got kicked. Then he heard who I was playing against and he said it was dangerous. And now he won't let me play. Not Mr Hope or Mr Bellow. My dad! My own dad won't let me play, so there!'

Then he went off.

So it wasn't Mr Hope making a favourite of Marky; it was Dribbler Wilson's dad being scared in case Dribbler got hurt!

'We could ask Dribbler's dad to let him play,' said Cyril.

'Let's see what happens on Saturday,' said Terence.

We put John Deacon in Peter Scott's place because he is a hard tackler, and we put Cyril and Harry in the middle of the back four. Scottie Watts took over from Marky. We put Marky alongside Harpur in the middle because he suddenly seemed to have started playing and anyway he is big. We put Daniel on the wing with

Peter Scott on the other side. The idea was that Daniel would pop up all over the place and support me. We thought we might get a few goals because both of us can hit the ball hard.

Abbey Villa had white shirts like Morth Heath and looked almost as big. Terence knew two of their players, Sam Corby and Dusker Jons, and Joe Fish of St Gabriel's said we had to watch out for one of their players, Cyril Ojke. Joe said Cyril was the fastest he'd played against, and he thought Abbey Villa would beat us.

'Thanks for nothing, Joe,' we said, and Cyril said afterwards that he thought Joe wanted to see us beaten because his team weren't in the Spring Cup, but I think Joe was trying to help. He was right about Cyril Ojke anyway.

We won the kick-off, and we had a Secret Kick-off Plan we had worked out in case we got the chance.

'Okay, Harpur?' I said, and Harpur nodded. So I gave the Secret Sign to Daniel.

Joe Small took the kick-off and played the ball to me and I back-heeled it to Harpur. I ran straight down the middle as fast as I could go. Harpur chipped the ball forward so that it would drop just around the edge of their area. It didn't bounce, though, because the moment I started running Daniel Rooney started running too, and he arrived inside their back and met the ball with his head, flicking it over the centre-half who had moved across for the through ball. Daniel's head-flick beat everyone and landed in my path. I hit a Super Shot and their goalie dived but couldn't get it!

1–0.

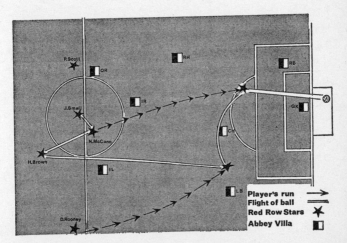

The diagram shows our move. We knew that they wouldn't have sorted out who was marking whom. Harpur had played a ball that would tempt the centre-half to go for it as well as the back, and Daniel, running in, got between them while they were making up their minds who should cut the ball out.

'Goal!' Cyril was jumping about and shouting as we lined up.

'Good goal,' Cyril Ojke said to me. 'You took that well.'

Then he started showing us what he could do!

First he outpaced Harry and Cyril in a race for the ball, and screwed it across the face of the goal. Terence yelled out 'Mine!' and then didn't come for the ball. Their winger cut inside and got in a header which John Deacon put behind for a corner. I could see Mr Hope holding his head in despair.

The corner came over. Harpur went to head clear and then BAM! Cyril Ojke got up above him and headed the ball down towards the foot of the post. Terence made a full-length one-handed save for another corner.

The corner came over and again Ojke went for it, but this time Terence called properly and came off his line to catch the ball. He spotted that Joe Small was free and threw a quick ball to him. Joe turned it out to Peter Scott and big Peter booted it on. I would have been through, but Sam Corby had come back to cut me out. Sam is tall and skinny, and he has a funny way of running as if he isn't fast, but he is. Sam got the ball and was holding it on the line, but I went in on him and the whistle went.

'Napper! Remember what I showed you!' Mr Hope called as I ran back. I nodded. Sam had been playing for the free kick to get himself out of an awkward position facing his own goal. I'd lunged in with my Napper McCann special tackle and done just what he wanted.

Then it was Ojke again. He got up to Sam's free kick and side-flicked the ball to Dusker Jons. Dusker quickly returned it behind Cyril, and Ojke went ghosting into our area and hit a delicate chip shot over Terence's head. The ball hit the underside of our crossbar and bounced down. Harry Haxwell slid in and turned it past the post for another corner kick.

I came back for the corner and positioned myself to block Sam Corby. I thought he might try a run from the back. The ball came over and all I saw was a blur of white shirt going past my shoulder.

Cyril Ojke launched himself at the ball, rising clear above everybody. It just skimmed over the bar with Terence beaten.

It was the same in every game. We were losing the battle when the ball was in the air because the other teams were bigger than we were.

'Wham, bang!' said Cyril Ojke, picking himself up from the ground and running back to the centre. All the teams we played against got the message quickly; put the ball over high and Red Row Stars are in trouble!

'We've got to do something about him. He's lightning!' Harpur said.

'Give him to Harry,' I said.

So we put Harry Haxwell on to marking Cyril Ojke.

That should have been all right; but as well as being a sort of lightning conductor when it came to getting up in the air, Cyril Ojke turned out to be a genius when the ball was on the ground. He could do anything he wanted with the ball, and the more Harry tried the sillier he began to look.

The fourth time it happened, Harry went banging on in, Cyril Ojke went down and the referee had a go at Harry.

From the free kick Ojke got in another of his headers, and our Cyril only managed to scrape it off the line into the path of their inside man who muffed it and shot past the post.

They were getting on top of us and Mr Hope was hopping up and down on the line and shouting to Harry and Cyril to get a grip on Ojke, and all the time Ojke was turning them inside out.

Terence took a goal kick. The ball went upfield and Joe Small played another of his one-twos with me. I was about to square the ball to Daniel when I heard Harpur calling, and instead of squaring the ball I flicked it sideways for Harpur to run on to. Harpur took the ball, dribbled up to Sam Corby, and played it back into my path. I hit it hard, and the ball struck their full-back and went bouncing back to their goalie. He bent down to pick it up and the ball bounced into his hands and out of them again – bounce, bounce, bounce – into the goal!

'Jeepers!' said Sam Corby, looking as if he'd just swallowed his pet ferret. (His dad, Percy Corby, keeps ferrets.)

2–0 to Red Row.

Two goals to Napper McCann, Super Striker.

I had scored two goals against Morth Heath and another that wasn't counted, and with that one I had five goals. Harry's penalty and Marky's old toe-punt that could have gone anywhere were our only other goals, so I was top scorer with five, though only four counted.

We thought we were going to be 2–0 up at half-time, but they went straight down to the other end and Cyril Ojke beat three men on his own. The ball went into the net like a rabbit into a hole. It was one of the greatest goals I have ever seen, even if it was against us!

'He should be in the England team,' I said to Dusker.

'Got an Under-13 trial,' Dusker said.

'Uh?' I said.

'Straight up,' said Dusker.

We kicked off, and then the whistle went.

'Dusker says Ojke got an England Under-13 trial,' I said to Terence as we were coming off.

'He's magic,' Terence said.

'Yes, but . . . under 13?' I said.

'Oh,' said Terence.

We told Mr Hope about it.

'County trial,' he said, 'not England. So what?'

'If he got an Under-13 county trial, what's he doing playing against us, Sir?' Terence said. 'He must be at the Big School then, mustn't he, Sir?'

'You're not in the Primary School League, Prince,' Mr Hope said.

Terence looked at me.

'What's the age limit in this one then, Sir?' Harpur asked, before I could say anything.

'Under 13,' said Mr Hope.

'But we haven't got anybody under 13!' I said. 'I mean, we're all under 13, but we haven't got anybody over 12, have we?'

It explained why all the other teams we had met seemed to be so big. We weren't in the Primary School League. We were in the Barnleck and District Spring Cup Under-13s!

'Think we'll win it now, Cyril?' I asked.

'Yes,' said Cyril.

It was funny but, when we went back on the field, the Abbey Villa team all looked much bigger than they had in the first half. I suppose it was because we knew most of them were older than us.

I went round reminding everyone that we were 2-1 up and would be third in the table, even if we were younger than all the other teams, and we cheered up.

It was their kick-off, and as soon as play started our Cyril went on to their Cyril Ojke. The idea was that Cyril would keep with him all the time, cut out everything that came to him and spoil him going for the ball. Everybody thought it was a great plan except Cyril – our Cyril, that is. Their Cyril didn't know anything about it until the game re-started.

He found out about it when Cyril cut out the first two passes Sam Corby played to him. The next one was in the air and Cyril – our Cyril – couldn't do anything about it. Cyril – their Cyril – got up above him and headed the ball sideways to their inside-left, who shot hard for the right hand corner of the goal, where Terence caught the ball with fly-paper hands.

Terence cleared the ball forward and Harpur got it and passed to Marky Bellow. Marky carried it on and fluffed his pass to me.

'Augh, Marky!' I shouted.

'Augh yourself, Napper!' he said, and he put his hands on his hips and glared at me.

The ball broke back and Ojke got it, but Cyril slide-tackled him before he could get settled on the ball. The ball broke loose again and Dusker got it. Dusker ran at John Deacon and beat him. Harry Haxwell came running across and launched himself in the air, feet first. Dusker knocked the ball to one side and Harry went sliding on by, leaving Dusker standing with his foot on the ball. Terence came running out. Dusker looked at him, and then scooped the ball clean over Terence's head and into goal.

This is Dusker's scoop shot in close-up. You can see the way he almost lifted the ball on his foot, and how well he is balanced:

2–2!

We kicked off again and the ball went up the field and Marky Bellow got it. He played a cross ball to Joe Small, but one of their midfield men cut it out and hit a long, hopeless, high ball into our area.

'My ball,' Terence called to Scottie Watts.

It was Terence's ball. There was nobody near him. But it didn't get to Terence because Scottie Watts went mad.

The ball was sailing over his head miles clear of everyone, and Scottie put his hands up above his head and caught it. Then he stood there, just inside our penalty area, looking silly.

Penalty!

We all looked sick.

We looked even sicker after Cyril Ojke hit it home. Two goals in two minutes.

'I thought you said catch it,' Scottie said to Terence.

Scottie had given away a silly goal for no reason, and we were 3–2 down in a game we had been winning!

We kicked off and lost the ball. They swept down on our goal again, and it looked like the game against Raven repeated!

Terence made two great saves and Ojke started getting on top of Cyril.

'You go and help Cyril, I'll stick with Harpur,' I said to big Marky. So Marky went back. He wasn't much of a footballer, but he had got the idea about putting his weight in the tackle and I hoped that the two of them could stop Ojke.

That was all right, but it didn't stop Dusker and Sam Corby. Sam started coming upfield now they were on top, and I found I had to leave the middle and mark him. Sam came further and further up, and that left a gap. 'If you get the ball, I'm going forward like a rocket,' I said to Harpur, but it didn't work out that way.

Marky Bellow took the ball off Ojke. He was so surprised at what he had done that he muffed his

kick, but luckily our Cyril got in quickly before
Ojke could recover and came out with the ball at
his feet.

'Use Daniel!' I shouted to Cyril, because I had
seen Daniel start off for the gap in the centre
where Sam Corby had been before he went
upfield.

Cyril played a perfect ball forward. Daniel
took it in his stride and beat their keeper with a
slick daisy-clipper that was a goal all the way.

3–3!

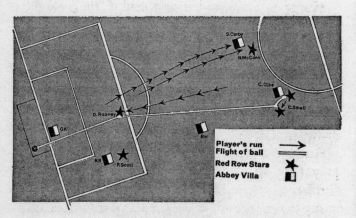

This is how we got the goal. You can see that
nobody had covered for Sam Corby, and Daniel
spotted the gap and hit his daisy-clipper before
the keeper could get close enough to him to
narrow the angle.

It was a great goal and we were all dancing
around pleased with ourselves.

We swarmed forward and got on to the attack. There were about five minutes to go and we were all over them. Our Cyril broke with the ball, their Cyril tackled him and there was a horrible crack sound as our Cyril fell over.

'Leave him! Leave him! Leave him!' shouted Mr Hope, sprinting on to the pitch.

Everybody clustered round Cyril and Mr Hope pushed us all back. Their Cyril came up to me and said, 'It wasn't my fault! It was fifty-fifty.'

'Okay,' I said.

Harry came up to me and said, 'It's broken.'

That was the first moment I realized what had happened.

Cyril's leg was broken.

The ambulance came and he went off to hospital.

'Three minutes to go,' said the ref. 'Call it a draw, shall we?'

And we all said yes, because nobody wanted to play football. The last thing I saw was their Cyril crying and Miss Fellows coming up to him to say that he wasn't to because it wasn't his fault.

BARNLECK AND DISTRICT
YOUTH LEAGUE

SPRING CUP: GROUP B

THIRD SERIES RESULTS

Red Row Stars 3   Abbey Villa 3
Skye Blues 4   Morth Park 3
Raven Boys Club 6   Morth Heath Youth 2

GROUP TABLE

Team	P	W	D	L	F	A	Pts
Skye Blues	3	3	0	0	16	7	6
Raven Boys Club	3	3	0	0	14	5	6
Abbey Villa	3	1	1	1	9	11	3
Red Row Stars	3	0	2	1	7	11	2
Morth Heath Youth	3	0	1	2	7	15	1
Morth Park	3	0	0	3	7	11	0

FIXTURES

Red Row Stars v. Morth Park
Raven Boys Club v. Skye Blues
Abbey Villa v. Morth Heath Youth

IMPORTANT NOTICE

Some clubs are still not fulfilling their obligation to communicate match results to the Match Secretary, 231 East Drive, Morth Park Estate by 8 p.m. Saturday.

This practice must cease or further steps will be taken.

C. Sefton, B.A. (Match Secretary)

6. Red Row Stars v. Morth Park

BARNLECK AND DISTRICT
YOUTH LEAGUE
SPRING CUP: GROUP B
Red Row Stars v. Morth Park
Referee: D. Kirk
Venue: Rec. field, Barnleck

Our game against Morth Park was one of our worst ever. Our team was all jumbled up and that is just the way we played!

'Harry has to take over the middle now we've lost Cyril,' Terence said. So Harry was the back man. Marky Bellow moved back from midfield to help him, and we moved John Deacon up from right-back to play alongside Harpur in midfield. That left a gap at right-back, so we had to move Peter Scott back there from outside-left, where he hadn't been doing anything anyway. We could have put Duncan Forbes at right-back, but we thought he was too small, so he went to outside-left.

'No sub,' Harpur pointed out.

'Helena Bellow!' said Cyril, but nobody laughed at his joke.

In the end we picked Jonathan Ramsey from the fourth year. Jonathan is tough, but he's no Dribbler Wilson.

This was the team we fielded against Morth Park for the last home match of our Spring Cup campaign. (We had three home matches and two away ones, like Raven Boys and Abbey Villa. Skye Blues and Morth Heath Youth and Morth Park had three away and two at home, so we were lucky that way.)

T. Prince

P. Scott   H. Haxwell   M. Bellow   S. Watts

D. Rooney   N. McCann (Capt.)   J. Small   D. Forbes

J. Deacon   H. Brown

Substitute J. Ramsey

Trainer Mr Hope

Travelling Official Miss E. Fellows

That was the team that we picked, but Miss Fellows couldn't come. She had to go shopping.

She didn't miss much.

We thought we would beat Morth Park because they were last in our Group with no points from their three games. If we beat them we would have four points; and if Raven Boys beat Skye Blues, Raven would be top with eight and Skye Blues would be two points in front of us with six. If we beat Skye Blues in our last game, we would be

72

equal with them on six points, but we might finish second on goal difference and then we would be in the semi-final against the winners of Group A. So it was absolutely essential that we beat the bottom team in the Group by a bagful of goals.

They were two goals up after ten minutes!

The first goal shouldn't have been a goal at all. Their winger hit a long ball from the wing. Terence was caught out of position and the wind blew it past him into the top corner of the net.

'Call yourself a keeper!' Harry said, picking the ball out of the net.

'Come on! Come on! They're no cop! We can win this one!' I shouted.

Then Marky Bellow put through his own goal. 2–0.

Then Harpur went up for a long ball, and their centre went up with him and somehow headed Harpur in the eye. Harpur had to go off and we brought on little Jonathan Ramsey. We put him on the left wing and moved Duncan Forbes back to Harpur's place, and Morth Park absolutely took over everything in the middle of the field. Harry and John Deacon were running around chasing shadows, and we could have been five down at half-time if it hadn't been for Terence.

Then Marky Bellow got kicked on the knee and had to go off. We were down to ten men.

'I'll go back,' Daniel said, and he went into midfield, where he had a great game, but it left me chasing the ball and coping more or less all on my own because I only had Jonathan Ramsey and Joe Small to pass to. Every time I passed to them they were knocked off the ball by the big Morth Park defenders.

Then John Deacon gave away a penalty. Terence got his hand to the penalty kick but couldn't stop it, and we were 3–0 down to the worst team in the Group.

Half-time: 3–0 to Morth Park.

'I feel like quitting!' Harry said, looking down in the mouth.

'Shut up, Harry,' I said. 'We're all in the same boat. We'll just have to have a go and win it, won't we?'

So in the second half Harry started coming forward and linking up with me.

I got away on the right and got a good shot in. Their keeper dived to his left and made a fantastic save. Then little Jonathan Ramsey got the ball within about a yard of goal and passed to one of their defenders!

They went down to the other end and Terence made two wonder saves in quick succession, one from Martin Routh and the other from a fat boy called Poncho.

Most of their players were drifting upfield now as they piled on the pressure. I knew that that was my chance, and I knew that Terence would be looking for me if he got a chance to hit a long ball that would give me a run.

The chance came when their back put in a high ball which Terence went for with Martin Routh. Terence got up above him and caught cleanly. When he came down Martin tried to crowd him, but Terence side-stepped him and hit a high ball downfield. The wind that had blown in their first goal was behind us now, and the ball beat their back four and left me in the clear with only the keeper to beat.

He came racing out of his area but I got to the ball first and flicked it past him. I hit it too hard and the ball was going wide of the goal when little Jonathan Ramsey got his foot to it. Their back tried a wild clearance and ballooned the ball in the air. I went for it and their keeper went for it, and he got his fist to the ball and punched out. Scottie Watts got the punch-out and toe-punted it towards the empty goal. One of their men headed out and the ball came to me. I lashed it into the net!

Goal!

Another Super Match Winner from N. McCann!

It really was the scrappiest old goal I have ever seen.

'Right!' I shouted. 'We're on our way! Come on, Stars! We've got to win this one!'

Some hope! They scored their fourth straight away after a good run by Martin Routh. 4–1 to Morth Park.

Harpur wanted to come on again, but the referee, Mr D. Kirk, said he couldn't come on because he had been substituted.

'But Marky had to go off as well,' I said. 'So we've only got ten men.'

'Sorry, son,' he said. 'Got to stick to the rules.'

He was right, but it didn't seem fair.

After that it became a boring old game. They were 4–1 up and we were down to ten men. It stayed like that till the end. We had lost to the bottom team in the Group and we were sick.

'Well?' Mr Hope said, in the dressing-room.

'Awful, Sir,' Terence said.

'Not good, no! But they played well. You thought it was going to be easy! You should have looked at their results.'

'They'd lost all their games, Sir!' Harry said. 'We're the only team they've beaten.'

'Whom did they lose to?' Mr Hope said.

He was right. They had lost to Skye Blues 4–3, to Raven 3–2 and to Abbey Villa 4–2. Raven had beaten us 5–1, and we had drawn with Abbey Villa, so it should have been a close game but for the injuries.

'Hard luck, lads!' the Morth Park Manager said, putting his head round the door. 'You gave us a good game.' Then he nodded at Mr Hope.

'You should get these lads some proper jerseys. They deserve 'em!' he said.

There was silence in the room after he had left.

'Our jerseys are proper,' Terence said.

It was his idea that we should all use our old school shirts and play in grey. It meant we would never have a colour clash. We had put plastic numbers on the back.

'Our football is the problem, not our jerseys,' said Harry.

Mr Hope cleared his throat. 'The shirts you made are fine,' he said. 'But just the same, I think you deserve a proper set. I've got a proposition for you!'

I looked up.

'Win your last game, and we will try and get you a set of jerseys. How about that?'

Nobody said anything.

'We can't win it,' Harry said.

'Yes, we can,' I said, although I thought Harry was right. I was supposed to be Captain, and if the Captain said we were beaten then everybody else would believe it and we *would* be beaten.

'There are a few things we'll have to sort out first,' Terence muttered after Mr Hope had gone out.

'Like signing the entire City First Team to play instead of us,' said Harpur.

'Like visiting a certain sweet-shop,' said Terence.

Which is how we came to be outside Wilson's sweet-shop after teatime, waiting for Mr Wilson to lock up.

Terence was spokesman.

When Mr Wilson came out and started putting on his bicycle clips, Terence very politely said, 'Good evening, Mr Wilson.'

Mr Wilson is a funny little baldy man, like Dribbler gone ancient. He looked at Terence over his glasses and said, 'I'm shut.'

'I am . . . I mean, we are . . . we are a deputation from Red Row Stars F.C.,' said Terence, trying to sound important.

'The school football team,' I said.

'Shut up, Napper,' said Harpur. 'Terence is doing the talking.'

'You're a deputation, are you?' said Mr Wilson. 'What do you want?'

'We want Dribbler to play in our next match, Mr Wilson,' said Terence. 'He's one of our best players and we have to win this match and Cyril can't play and we're going to lose it if we haven't got Dribbler.'

'Cyril can't play?' mused Mr Wilson.

'Cyril br-OUCH!' Harpur kicked me just in time to stop me saying 'Cyril broke his leg', which wouldn't have been a very smart thing to say.

'We need Dribbler, Sir,' said Terence. 'I know he's a bit small for the teams we're playing against. But he is *brilliant*. We'll put him on the wing where he won't get kicked too much . . .'

'At all,' said Harpur quickly.

'Much,' I said.

'Not very much,' said Terence.

'Donald's brilliant?' said Mr Wilson, doubtfully.

'It's very important,' said Terence, and he told Mr Wilson why it was very important. Mr Wilson got on his bicycle and said, 'I'll speak to his mother', and rode off. We didn't know whether he was on our side or not.

BARNLECK AND DISTRICT YOUTH LEAGUE

SPRING CUP: GROUP B

FOURTH SERIES RESULTS
Red Row Stars 1   Morth Park 4
Raven Boys Club 3   Skye Blues 5
Abbey Villa 4   Morth Heath Youth 4

GROUP TABLE

Team	P	W	D	L	F	A	Pts
Skye Blues	4	4	0	0	21	10	8
Raven Boys Club	4	3	0	1	17	10	6
Abbey Villa	4	1	2	1	13	15	4
Morth Park	4	1	0	3	11	12	2
Red Row Stars	4	0	2	2	8	15	2
Morth Heath Youth	4	0	2	2	11	19	2

FIXTURES
Skye Blues v. Red Row Stars
Morth Heath Youth v. Morth Park
Abbey Villa v. Raven Boys Club

IMPORTANT IMPORTANT IMPORTANT IMPORTANT

ALL match results to Match Secretary by 8 p.m. Saturday at latest.

The practice of making late returns CANNOT be allowed to continue.

C. Sefton B.A. (Match Secretary)

7. Tactics

Mr Wilson came down on his bicycle halfway through training on Wednesday night, and when he went away Mr Hope came across to us and said, 'You didn't tell me you were going on a deputation.' He didn't sound very pleased.

'It was only us, Sir, the Selection Committee, not the others. We wanted our best team, Sir, and Dribbler should be in it, Sir, shouldn't he?'

'Well, he will be,' said Mr Hope.

We all started cheering.

'But don't go approaching parents again without my permission, please,' he said. 'The school is already in enough trouble over this football.'

We looked at each other.

'What trouble, Sir?' we said.

'Never mind,' he said.

Then he told us all to get changed and to come into the main hall to talk about Saturday's match. And when we did, two people came in whom we hadn't been expecting. One was Miss Fellows and the other was Cyril, with his leg all covered in plaster.

'Ah,' said Mr Hope. 'My spies!'

Then he told us what Miss Fellows had been doing on Saturday when she had told us she was going shopping. She hadn't gone shopping at all. She had taken Cyril in her car on a top secret spying mission to see Skye Blues beating Raven Boys Club 5–3.

'Oh,' said Dribbler. 'We're all going to get dosey-whatsits on the men we're marking!'

'That won't be necessary,' said Miss Fellows.

'The point is,' said Mr Hope, 'that now we know the men we have to stop.'

He got Cyril to bang his plaster leg up on to the hall platform and tell us all about it. Cyril said they were a good, big team with a lot of strong players, but they didn't play a lot of football. Instead they relied on three players to win matches for them. The first was their striker Herd. 'He's small, but very quick. You have to watch him anywhere round the box,' said Cyril. Then they had two midfield men, Karnos and Oldfield. Karnos was strong, and loved to come forward. Oldfield was very solid and great in the air. We had to watch for him at set pieces. They had two useful wingers, both of whom could put across a good centre, and a boy called Hampton who did a lot of heading near goal. 'The good thing is that Herd can't do much in the air,' said Cyril. 'But he makes up for it on the ground.'

'What about their defence?' I said. 'If we're going to get a result, we'll have to do some attacking.'

Cyril said their defence was their weak spot.

'They're so used to attacking and winning games that they come forward too much. The whole thing revolves around Oldfield. If you can get him drawn, the rest aren't up to much. There's one other thing that ought to suit us,' said Cyril, and then he gave a grin. 'They like to play offside!'

'Oh,' Harpur said.

'Well, we've got the players to take that on, haven't we?' said Mr Hope. 'The two nippiest strikers in the competition.'

He meant Daniel Rooney and me.

'So we'll be relying on you boys at the back to feed the ball forward fast in front of Rooney and McCann, in the hope that their defence will try to spring the offside and get it wrong,' said Mr Hope. 'We'll have to tighten things up at the back and cut down on goalkeeping errors, eh, Prince?'

'What about Herd?' said Harry. 'If I've got to take this guy Hampton in the air and their wingers are good crossers of the ball, I won't be able to cut Herd out.'

'I could take him, Sir,' said Harpur.

Mr Hope shook his head. 'We're relying on you to be up and down the field, attacking and defending. We can't have you pinned down. Anyway, we won't adjust our whole team to them. They must adjust to us! If you can get enough through balls going to McCann and

Rooney, you won't have to worry about Herd.'

'But who is going to mark him, Sir?' asked Harry.

'Deacon can pick him up,' said Mr Hope. 'At least, Deacon can do it when he's near goal. But that isn't enough. I don't want this young man getting a chance to settle on the ball at all. That's why I'm going to bring Small back.'

'Cyril can't play,' Dribbler said. 'He's got a broken leg.'

'Joe,' said Mr Hope. 'Not Cyril.'

'I'm not much of a tackler, Sir,' said Little Joe.

'You don't have to be,' said Mr Hope. 'I want you to ignore the play. I want you to go out on the field, get within two feet of Herd, and stay there. Every time the ball comes to him he'll have you right on top of him. One rule only, Joseph. Stay between Herd and our goal. If he has to go past you, he'll have to play the ball on and that should give Deacon his chance.'

'I see,' said Joe, looking doubtful.

'Doesn't matter if he beats you,' said Mr Hope. 'Keep after him. Spoil him. Get in his way. Don't foul him or kick him or talk at him. Just stay with him. If he goes off the field for an orange, go with him. On his heels all the time. You're his doggie for the day! Deacon can do the serious business of tackling him. You're there to annoy him.'

That was great. It left only a small problem, like two wingers who were both useful and could put in a cross!

'Bellow on one. Watts on the other,' said Mr Hope. 'Rooney and Wilson to double back and help them out.'

'What about Karnos coming from the back, Sir?' said Cyril. 'He's big and he's strong and he loves to come forward.'

'He's going to have a battle with Harpur Brown, isn't he?' said Mr Hope. 'Brown versus Karnos, for the middle of the field. That could decide the game.'

'I'll give him a run for his money,' said Harpur.

'We're going to win this one,' said Mr Hope, rubbing his hands.

'We are the Champions,' shouted Cyril, and he banged his plaster cast on the floor.

'Trouble is, we're not the Champions,' I said to Terence and Harpur when we were walking home. 'We're equal with two clubs on two points each. They're playing each other, and we're playing the top team in the group. Our goal difference is -7. Morth Park have -1 and Morth Heath -8. If we lose, and they draw with each other, they both go above us and we finish bottom. Even if they don't draw, the team that loses its game will probably have a better goal difference than we'll have after we've played Skye Blues.'

'We'd have to beat Skye Blues 6–0 to equal Morth Park,' Harpur said. '6–0!'

'They're more likely to beat us 6–0,' I said.

'Then we're bottom of the Group.'

'And Miss Fellows is in trouble,' said Terence.

'Why?'

'That's what Mr Hope meant. Miss Fellows put us in the Under-13s. She shouldn't have. Some of the parents complained, we know that, and people said the Barnleck and District was too tough for us. Now Cyril has broken his leg and we look like finishing bottom and everyone will blame Miss Fellows, won't they?'

'Oh,' I said.

'I'll tell you what we're going to do about it,' said Terence. 'I don't care if the Skye Blues are top of the Group. We're going to go out there and beat them!'

8. Skye Blues v. Red Row Stars

**BARNLECK AND DISTRICT
YOUTH LEAGUE**
SPRING CUP: GROUP B
Skye Blues v. Red Row Stars
Referee: K. J. Stallard
Venue: Old Field Carnley

This was the Red Row Stars team which took the field for our vital last match against Skye Blues:

T. Prince

M. Bellow   H. Haxwell   J. Deacon   S. Watts

P. Scott   H. Brown

D. Rooney   N. McCann (Capt.)   J. Small   D. Wilson

Substitute D. Forbes

Trainer Mr Hope

Travelling Official Miss E. Fellows

Spy C. Small

That was the way we wrote the team out, but not the way we intended to play. Marky Bellow and Daniel Rooney were going to cut out the winger on the right side of the defence, with Scottie Watts and Dribbler Wilson doing the same job on the left. We reckoned that that would cut down on the supply of balls to Hampton and Herd. Hampton would have Harry Haxwell competing in the air for every ball; and when he laid it off to Herd, Herd would find Joe Small and John Deacon snapping at his heels, hunting in a pack. If Harpur could win his fair share of the midfield from Karnos, it would be my job to take on Oldfield and his offside trap and win the game for Red Row.

The Skye Blues looked like real professionals in their striped shirts. We kicked off and about a minute later it started to rain. The ground was hard to begin with and the rain made the surface slippery, which helped us and didn't help their big defenders.

I got the ball and fed Dribbler Wilson. Dribbler turned the ball outside the back and beat him to the touch-line, then he curled the ball in. I went up with the keeper, but the keeper got the ball. I closed in on him and the whistle went.

'Ouch, ref!' I said, and turned round to speak to him.

Then I saw who the ref was.

K. J. Stallard! – the ref who had nearly sent me off for worrying the goalie against Morth Heath Youth when I hadn't even touched the keeper!

He gave me a finger-wagging and left me in no doubt that he remembered me!

'I'll be watching you, son,' he said, and ran back for the free kick.

'Forget about the keeper, Napper,' Harpur said as we went back. 'The game isn't worth the candle!'

The free kick was a huge one, and the wind carried it right to the edge of our box where Hampton got up above Harry and headed down to Herd. Herd controlled the ball and slipped it past Joe Small as Joe stuck out his foot. John Deacon got in a tackle and the ball broke to the left where Hampton got a foot to it and sent it for a goal kick.

'Come on, Harry!' I shouted. 'You've got to get the high ones.'

The next ball to the middle, Harry got up above Hampton, but the ref said Harry had climbed on him and gave a free kick.

Herd took the free kick.

Here is our line-up as we faced it. You can see that Scottie Watts hadn't covered properly. Herd saw it too.

He hit the ball like a bullet and Terence dived brilliantly to his right and got a fist to it. The ball went to their inside-right who swung it in the air to the far post where Marky Bellow chested it down and lost control. Big Karnos came running in to blast it into our net. He drew back his foot to crash the ball home and Terence arrived out of nowhere, blocking the ball with his body and somehow holding onto it.

'Great save, that,' said Oldfield.

I was lying up close to him by the halfway line. He had waved his backs forward and Karnos had already gone upfield, so the long run was on if I could get the ball.

Terence laid it out to Harpur, and Harpur played the ball across the field to Daniel Rooney. Daniel controlled it, side-stepped one man, and saw me heading for the wing where the space was clear.

'Daniel!' I called.

But he didn't release the ball. Instead he ran inside, heading for Oldfield. I stopped. Then Daniel hit the ball to where I would have been if I'd kept going.

'Napper!' he shouted in disgust.

Karnos picked up the ball in midfield. He came forward, beat Harpur, and fired in a great shot which Terence held in a full-length dive down by the foot of the post.

Herd went in and the ref's whistle went. He started talking to Herd.

'Herdy never touched your keeper,' Oldfield muttered to me.

'Old Stallard is like that,' I said. 'He chased me round the field one day against the Heath.'

'He's a nutter,' said Oldfield.

Karnos beat Harpur in the air when the free kick came downfield. This time he laid it off for Oldfield. Oldfield went forward and hit a thirty-yard screamer that nicked off the top of the cross-bar with Terence beaten.

'You've struck lucky today,' Karnos muttered.

Daniel Rooney got the ball. Again I started a run and again he didn't release it quickly enough, and in the end I was given offside.

Every time the ball came through, all I could hear was Oldfield calling 'Out! Out!' and the whistle going.

The trouble was that my supply of the ball should have been coming from Harpur, but big Karnos was pressing so far upfield that Harpur was pushed back and I wasn't getting any play.

Then Dribbler Wilson got past the back against the touch-line and screwed the ball across. Daniel came inside me and had a shot which almost broke the corner flag.

'Give me an early ball or two, Daniel,' I said to him.

'Don't keep stopping,' he said.

Offside is always difficult to play against till you get used to it.

We were getting used to it.

I didn't get clear but Daniel did. One of Marky Bellow's stupid toe-punters found him on his own and he cut off for goal. Their goalie came out and dived at his feet. The ball broke loose and Oldfield played it for a corner just before I could reach it.

Secret Sign Number Six.

The Short Corner Plan!

I went to the near post and Harpur moved up at the back, with big Karnos following him.

Daniel hit a perfect short centre and I ran forward and back-headed the ball. Harpur and Karnos rose for it. Harpur got a touch and the ball was in the top corner of the net! Here is the goal:

Karnos should have got it, because he is taller than Harpur, but Harpur had timed his run well and got up over him. It was a brilliant goal for Red Row Stars!

We were 1–0 in front.

They went mad!

They were top of the Group and they had been winning all their games and scoring lots of goals, and we were almost bottom and we were beating them 1–0 due to Secret Plan Number Six. It was a good Plan to use because Oldfield was too tall to be beaten in the air on an ordinary corner. But by playing the ball short, what mattered was getting to it first, and I did that.

They really came at us after our goal, but Terence was playing like an England International!

They got a corner and when it came over, Terence shouted 'Mine' and went up with Hampton and took the ball off his head, as if he had been catching corners like that all season instead of dropping them.

He hit the ball forward.

It was a long, long ball, on a wet and windy day. Oldfield went for it, and the ball skidded off the grass under his foot.

He tried to get back, but I surged past him. The keeper came rushing out. Daniel called, 'Napper.' I pushed the ball sideways and Daniel came sprinting in and knocked it into the net as easy as pie.

2–0 to Red Row Stars!

Cyril was dancing up and down on the line, banging everyone with his plaster until Mr Hope told him to be sensible! Miss Fellows was grinning all over her face.

Herd lined up at outside-left.

'Let him go, Johnny,' Mr Hope shouted to John Deacon. 'You stay with him, Joe.' So Joe Small moved across to the right.

Then Mr Hope shouted to Marky that he was to pick up Herd.

The ball came down the middle and Hampton headed it down, but their outside-left who had come into the centre wasn't quick enough to pick it out. Harry Haxwell got the ball and played it back to Terence.

Terence threw the ball to Dribbler, and Dribbler lost it in a tackle to Karnos who came forward and tried another of his shots, but shot wide.

'We want three! We want three!' Cyril and Duncan Forbes were chanting on the line, and Cyril started hitting the bucket with his plaster cast until Mr Hope stopped him.

Skye Blues swept forward again. Herd got the ball and beat Marky and Joe Small in a race to the line. He screwed the ball across and Terence came racing out. Hampton crashed into him and Mr K. J. Stallard gave his usual free kick for breathing on goalies, although this time I think it really was a foul.

I got clear from the free kick but mistimed the ball, and Oldfield beat me and fed Karnos. Karnos came forward and beat Harpur again. He was beating Harpur most of the time by now. He delayed his shot and then didn't shoot at all, but drifted the ball across the goalmouth.

Herd was the one who couldn't head the ball, according to Cyril.

Herd came racing in and took off in a headlong dive. He met the ball at the edge of the goal area and smacked it firmly with his forehead and Terence made the SAVE OF THE CENTURY! Here he is making it:

'I give up,' said Oldfield.

Then they broke away again down the left. Herd hit a curling ball into the far post and Hampton got up and headed past Terence into the bottom corner.

2–1 to Red Row Stars.

Half-time!

'Well done, boys,' said Mr Hope. Then he started talking about the second half. The first thing he did was to switch Harpur and Harry. Karnos was beating Harpur to the ball, and Hampton was winning in the air against Harry. 'You must cut Karnos out. He could have had a hat-trick!' Mr Hope said. Then he clapped Terence on the back and said what a brilliant goalie he was, but that he wasn't to forget to come out for the high balls against Hampton because Harpur would have his hands full. He told Daniel Rooney to release the ball quicker and he told me to start shouting.

'Get into the game, Napper,' he said. 'You look like you're taking a nap out there!'

'Okay,' I said, but I was annoyed. He wouldn't let me go back to help, and with Harpur in trouble against Karnos there had been no one to give me balls to move on to. In the second half I would be depending on Harry, and that would make things even worse.

Skye Blues came out for the second half looking very determined. They wanted to finish top of the Group. Straight from the whistle Harry and Karnos got into a tangle and the ref, Mr K. J. Stallard, rushed over and did one of his orchestral pieces sorting them out. Then he gave a free kick against Harry.

Karnos took the free kick and played it into our area. Hampton stroked it on. Herd took it on his chest, dropped the ball on to his instep and flicked it just inside the post for a brilliant goal!

Here is Herd playing the ball. You can see the
way he played it high on his chest and shaped
himself to flick it home.

'Told you he was good,' Cyril said, looking
mournful.

2–2.

They had come right back into the game. Our
lead was gone and they looked like winning, because they were all over us.

Herd was moving about the midfield instead of
lurking up front, trying to draw people out to
mark him. Joe Small kept trotting after him and
getting in his way, so that part of the plan was
working well.

What we hadn't counted on was that Hampton would be as good as he was. We expected him
to get the ball in the air a lot because every team
we had played against had managed that, but we
didn't expect him to use it so well. The teams who
had played us before had beaten us in the air,
because they were older and taller than we were,

and then wasted the ball. Hampton was able to place the ball exactly where he wanted it.

'Close up on the wingers! Close up on the wingers!' Mr Hope shouted. 'Cut off his supply.'

What happened was that Scottie and Mark tried to close up on the wingers and follow them around the way Joe Small was following Herd. The difference was that Joe Small always had somebody else to back him up.

The outside-left went past Marky three times. Each time he got his cross in we were at panic stations. Luckily, nothing came of them. But Marky was getting into such trouble that Daniel had to go back, and it was one of his trips to help the defence that gave away a goal.

Herd got the ball with his back to goal and Joe came in. Herd dummied him and Joe bought the dummy. John Deacon was late in his tackle and Herd nipped inside him and hit a screamer for goal. Terence dived and missed the ball and Daniel stuck out his fist and punched it over the bar.

Mr K. J. Stallard was very cross. He took Daniel's name and threatened to send him off. Then he put the ball on the penalty spot.

Terence has a special trick for penalty kicks. He stands a little to one side of his goal, hoping that the penalty taker will think he has made a mistake. When the penalty kicker hits the ball to the unguarded side, Terence is able to make a great save.

Karnos took the kick.

I have never seen anyone hit the ball so hard.

It didn't matter where Terence was; the ball crashed into the net.

3–2 down.

We were losing, and we were going to be last in the Group and all the parents would say we shouldn't have been in it. Miss Fellows would be in trouble over Cyril's broken leg and all our kicks and bruises.

I suppose we shouldn't have been in an Under-13 competition anyway. We were too small.

Then I decided that we weren't.

'Come on, Red Row!' I shouted.

Nobody shouted with me.

Cyril was standing on the line with a face like cold pudding. Harry was muttering under his breath.

I got the ball and ran through and beat the keeper and missed the goal by a mile.

'We've had it, Napper,' Harry said to me.

'No, we haven't. I nearly got one there,' I said.

They went back on the attack and Karnos came racing through and fired a great shot into the corner of the net, but the referee gave a free kick for a foul on Harry. It is unusual for anyone to foul Harry. Usually Harry does the fouling.

From the free kick Dribbler got the ball, and this time he turned inside, beating the back again.

He moved towards Karnos and feigned to pass the ball to me, but instead switched his feet and slipped it past Karnos. I went screaming down the middle and Dribbler looked up, saw the goalie moving to come out, and chipped the ball neatly over his head into the net.

GOAL!

3–3.

We were holding on for a draw, after we had just about looked beaten!

The rain came on again and the ground began to get heavier, which didn't help our smaller players, but it did slow down their wingers a bit too. The left wing got boggy and they couldn't get the ball over to Hampton's head so easily. Harpur was beating him now and then as well, which helped, and Terence came out for two crosses. He made a muck of his punch on one of them, but luckily Herd swiped at the ball and missed it. I wasn't the only one who could miss open goals.

'We've only got to hold it and we've got a draw,' Harry said.

He was chasing Karnos all over the place and managing to keep a much better hold on him than Harpur had, which slowed up their attack. As the minutes went by, Oldfield started to venture up as well.

'Stay where you are,' Harpur called to me when I signalled to him about moving back.

Harpur got the ball in a tussle with Herd. He found Daniel, who turned the ball behind Oldfield. I ran on to it and I was clear, but the ref gave offside.

'Keep it tight! Keep it tight!' Karnos shouted; but he wasn't helping to keep it tight, he was up there trying to get his name on the score sheet.

They swept forward again. Terence got down to a drive from Karnos by the near post and pulled off a great save. Then they got a free kick on the edge of our area, and Karnos took it.

Oldfield had moved up for the set piece, and this time I went with him because Cyril had warned us that he was dynamite in dead-ball situations.

Karnos floated the ball over. Oldfield went up for it and I went up with him. He got up over me and headed it down. The ball bounced towards the goal, and Terence went down clawing and slithering after it and turned it against the post. The ball came off the post and Marky Bellow booted it. It went out to their back, who fired in a great shot.

I saw it coming at me, and I jumped as high as I could and headed the ball. It went up into the air and over the bar. I had saved a certain goal on our goal-line with a Fantastic Napper McCann Super Header!

I stayed back for the corner and it came swinging over. Hampton went for the ball and Terence called that it was his and we left it. Terence went up and the wet ball skidded through his gloves and hit Peter Scott on the knee. It dribbled past the post for another corner.

The second corner came over and Terence and Harpur and Hampton went up for it. Terence punched out and Karnos got the ball and fired it in. It hit Marky in the stomach and Marky went over on his back holding his stomach. The ball broke free and John Deacon turned it for another corner.

Three corners, one after the other.

The ball came over. Terence went for it again and caught it cleanly.

I was running.

Oldfield was out of position.

Terence threw the ball hard and low, but he threw it badly. Karnos came sweeping across to knock it clear and Joe Small somehow appeared from nowhere, slid in front of him and turned the ball into my path.

I booted the ball on and kept on running with their full-back converging on me. I got to the ball first and saw Daniel Rooney coming up on the left, so I screwed it to him and he hit in a screamer. Their goalie went right across his goal and caught the ball at full stretch. Then he got up and cleared the ball quickly as his defence came back.

'Out! Out!' Oldfield yelled. The defenders started moving forward.

The goalkeeper made a bad clearance. Harry beat Karnos to the ball and hooked it back towards goal.

The defenders were caught moving out, and I was through them like a hot knife through butter with the ball in my path and only the keeper to beat.

I hit the ball a great Napper McCann Screamer from twenty yards and it ripped past the goalie's hand and crashed into the net!

4–3 to Red Row Stars!

A magnificent winner from Napper McCann, Superstar!

Here is the goal. You can see how Harry's quick through ball beat their defence as they moved out:

Skye Blues forgot about defending!

Oldfield, Karnos, Herd, Hampton, the two wingers – they hit us with everything they had. They could see the title of Group B Winners slipping away from them, and they didn't like it!

Terence made three brilliant saves from Karnos and Oldfield and Herd, and then, right in the last minute, Herd beat Joe Small and me, and ghosted into the area.

Terence came dashing out and spread himself as Herd shot.

The ball struck him on the shoulder and spun up into the air. Herd crashed after it and got in a header and Harry Haxwell, back on the line covering, somehow spooned the ball off the line. The right-winger scraped it back instead of letting it go for a corner and Terence, on his knees, managed to push it up in the air again. I dived in, got a foot to the ball, and it went into touch.

Then the whistle went.

4–3 to Red Row Stars!

We had won our greatest-ever victory and taken two points off the League leaders in a Smashing Upset-Of-The-Season Win!

BARNLECK AND DISTRICT YOUTH LEAGUE.

FIFTH SERIES RESULTS

Skye Blues 3   Red Row Stars 4
Morth Heath Youth 2   Morth Park 6
Abbey Villa 2   Raven Boys Club 6

GROUP TABLE

Team	P	W	D	L	F	A	Pts
Raven Boys Club	5	4	0	1	23	12	8
Skye Blues	5	4	0	1	24	14	8
Morth Park	5	2	0	3	17	14	4
Abbey Villa	5	1	2	2	15	21	4
Red Row Stars	5	1	2	2	12	18	4
Morth Heath Youth	5	0	2	3	13	25	2

FIXTURES

Spring Cup semi-finals
Skye Blues v. Crown Club
Donneycore v. Raven Boys Club

IMPORTANT

Future match results should be communicated to
P. Carragher, 11 Downs Road, Barnleck. Match
Secretary C. Sefton has resigned due to pressure
of work.

9. A New Challenge

That's how our Super Great Victory over the Skye Blues stopped us coming bottom of our Group and made Avril and Ugly Irma Bankworth look silly, because they had been going around saying that we were no good and would never beat anybody.

Well, we did.

We competed in the Barnleck and District Spring Cup, which is for Under-13s, not Primary Schools, and we might have won it if it hadn't been for bad luck.

We beat the Skye Blues. In the semi-finals the Skye Blues beat the winners of Group A, Crown Club, and then they won 7–6 on penalties in the final against Donneycore. We were the only team to beat the team that won the competition, and we might have won it ourselves if Cyril hadn't broken his leg. The other thing we were pleased about was Morth Heath Youth finishing bottom, which served them right. They were the worst footballers in the group, and the toughest when it came to kicking people instead of the ball.

Mr Hope got us new red jerseys, with yellow numbers and a badge like a star for Red Row

Stars. Miss Fellows got our names down for the Primary Schools League.

'There's a new challenge for you!' Mr Hope said. 'See if you can win it.'

Winning it would mean beating our great rivals, the Stringy Pants of St Gabriel's, and all the other Primary Schools round Myreton and Barnleck.

'Reckon we can do it?' I asked Cyril.

'Reckon we can do *anything*,' said Cyril.

Then we all cheered, and kept on cheering, because we had a great team and we were going straight to the top!

Red Row Stars: Summary of Appearances and Goalscorers

BARNLECK AND DISTRICT SPRING CUP: GROUP B

v. *Morth Heath Youth* (Home)
Team: T. Prince   P. Scott   C. Small
H. Haxwell   J. Deacon   S. Watts   H. Brown
S. Rodgers   N. McCann   J. Small   D. Wilson
Sub: D. Forbes
Result: 3–3   *Goalscorers: McCann 2*
Haxwell 1 (P)

v. *Raven Boys Club* (Away)
Team: T. Prince   P. Scott   C. Small
J. Deacon   M. Bellow   N. McCann   H. Brown
S. Rodgers   H. Haxwell   J. Small   D. Forbes
Sub: D. Rooney   Rooney for Rodgers
Result: 1–5   Goalscorer: Bellow

v. *Abbey Villa* (Home)
Team: T. Prince   J. Deacon   C. Small
H. Haxwell   S. Watts   M. Bellow   H. Brown
D. Rooney   N. McCann   J. Small   P. Scott
Sub: D. Forbes
Result: 3–3   Goalscorers: McCann 2
Rooney 1

v. *Morth Park* (Home)
Team: T. Prince   P. Scott   H. Haxwell
M. Bellow   S. Watts   J. Deacon   H. Brown
D. Rooney   N. McCann   J. Small   D. Forbes
Sub: J. Ramsey   Ramsey for Brown
Result: 1–4   Goalscorer: McCann

v. *Skye Blues* (Away)
Team: T. Prince   M. Bellow   H. Haxwell
J. Deacon   S. Watts   P. Scott   H. Brown
D. Rooney   N. McCann   J. Small   D. Wilson
Sub: D. Forbes
Result: 4–3   Goalscorers: Brown   Rooney
Wilson   McCann

Football Notes

by Ms E. Fellows

The School Team, Red Row Stars, took part in its first proper competition this term. Unfortunately our players had to compete against boys in an older age-group and, on this occasion, we did not win the Cup! A number of players showed considerable improvement on past form, and I feel that, given competition with boys of appropriate age and size, we can look forward to future triumphs on the soccer field!

The following players took part:

Prince, Terence Our excellent and agile keeper found some difficulty in coping with the aggressive approach of some of the players we met. Terence's form has been a little erratic this season, but he came back to confidence in the last game, when at times he stood alone!

Bellow, Mark Has come on considerably this term after a shaky start. We were delighted to see his name on the score-sheet this term. Must learn to kick properly.

Haxwell, Harold Harry is a strong player, inclined to be over-robust on occasion. When he learns to control himself he will make a greater contribution to the team.

Deacon, John A very busy player, John has made considerable progress this term despite lack of stature.

Watts, Andrew 'Scottie' has had a poor term. He needs to apply himself more to the game. Apt to be slow on the turn and easily discouraged.

Scott, Peter Peter has tried hard, but made little impact.

Brown, Harpur Harpur has played with distinction throughout the term. His heading ability against larger boys has been a revelation. Harpur will one day make a very fine player indeed if he maintains his present rate of progress.

Rooney, Daniel A non-starter last term due to illness, Daniel came into the team and made an instant impact. Sometimes shoots when he could pass to a better-placed colleague. A strong and active player.

McCann, Bernard 'Napper' is sometimes inclined to 'nap' a little on the pitch and fade out of the game. Our leading goalscorer and Captain, he is a deadly finisher. His tackling could improve.

Small, Joseph Playing against much bigger boys, he has displayed great courage.

Wilson, Donald 'Dribbler' was missing from the team due to untoward circumstances for much of the season. He has natural ability and can take on an opponent and beat him at will.

Small, Cyril Our cheerleader unfortunately suffered injury in mid-term. A keen and enthusiastic player, he made his contribution off the field as well as on.

Ramsey, Jonathan Came in for one game this term. Small, but determined.

Rodgers, Scudamore Has temporarily dropped out of the team. Too easily discouraged, Scudamore will need to show more interest if he is to regain his place.

Forbes, Duncan Came in for two games this term. A small but useful player.

Our thanks are due to our caretaker, Mr Hogan, for opening the hall, and to all the parents who contributed towards the new set of jerseys. Mr Hope has taken over team training, and this innovation has been welcomed by all, not least the writer.

We expect to make a real challenge for honours in the Primary School League next term.

Ms E. Fellows